CONTENTS

Chapter 1

The First Rehearsal

When you live by the seaside, summer holidays are all about ice creams and sandcastles and hunting for pirate gold. My mum and dad have to work during the holidays this year, so my gran is looking after me, which I have been looking forward to. Gran and I are really close and she is great at hunting for treasure. One time we found an ancient fossil on the beach, which I still keep on my bedside table.

But things haven't worked out the way I planned.

Instead of playing on the beach, here I am with my gran and two old ladies who are having a fight over a bright orange wig.

"Give it here, Denise!" the first old lady yells.

"Give over, Freda, you know orange is not your colour!" the second lady squawks in reply.

Denise and Freda are Gran's friends. They are part of her drama club, and they are putting on *Cinderella* at the old theatre on the seafront.

Gran says that if loads of people come to see the play, they will be able to save the theatre. It's in danger as the council want to close it down. It needs a lot of repairs and the council say they don't have any money for this. Gran loves the theatre and says it is a local treasure and an important part of the town's history.

I don't know about that … it feels a bit dark and dirty to me these days, as if no one has looked after it properly. The floorboards creak and the red velvet seats are worn thin. The red and gold paint around the stage is chipped.

Don't get me wrong, I do like the theatre, and I want to spend time with Gran, but the problem is that right now I want to be on the beach. And I can even hear an ice-cream truck outside.

But Gran thinks it's a good idea if I help out with rehearsals. Worse than that, Gran wants *me* to play the part of Cinderella. But there is no way I'm doing it. Does Gran even know about stage fright? I don't think Gran is afraid of anything. But I am. Just thinking about being on stage makes my heart thump fast and my hands go all clammy.

"Come on, Callie! It will be something fun for us to do together," Gran says with a big grin so I can see her lovely, shiny false teeth. (Gran is very proud of her false teeth, and I have to admit they do look like movie-star teeth because they're very big and square and white.)

I don't want to hurt Gran's feelings, so I've come along to meet the GOLDEN OLDIES DRAMA SOCIETY (or G.O.D.S., as they call themselves). Even that gives me butterflies in my tummy, but so far the rehearsal has been very boring. Not only are Denise and Freda having a fight

over who gets to wear the bright orange wig, but a very grumpy man called Norman keeps forgetting his lines.

"No, Norman dear," Gran says (because Gran is the director), "the line is 'I WANT EVERY WOMAN IN THE KINGDOM TO TRY ON THIS SLIPPER'."

"That's what I said," Norman huffs.

"Oh no it isn't!" Denise shouts from the side of the stage.

"I'm afraid you said you wanted everyone to try on a KIPPER," Gran explains to Norman.

"I did no such thing." Norman's cheeks go red. "I think I know the difference between a slipper and a kipper!"

"Let's just try again, shall we?" Gran asks.

Norman walks slowly off the stage and then walks slowly back on again. "I WANT EVERY WOMAN IN THE KINGDOM TO TRY ON THIS KIPPER!" he shouts, holding up an old yellow flip-flop.

I make a snorting sound as I try not to laugh.

Norman's face goes an even darker red. "Well, now you've put the idea in my head!" he groans. "If you hadn't said anything about kippers, then everything would have been fine."

"Let's take it from the top," Gran says with a jolly grin.

I sit back in my seat and sigh. I think it's going to be a very long day.

Chapter 2

A Fairy-Tale Forest

The fairy godmother in Gran's *Cinderella* play is a lady called Pamela. She has a lot of pink blusher on her cheeks and her eyelashes are long and dark like spiders' legs. Her white hair has been dyed a funny pale pink colour that is a bit like candy floss. I think it is pretty cool.

Pamela told me that the fairy godmother is the *real* star of the show, not "that wet Cinderella girl," she said. That cheered me up. Maybe it won't be so bad being in the play if I don't have to be the star. But I still really don't want to do it. And, maybe Pamela is right ... maybe Cinderella is a bit lame anyway.

When I was little, I sometimes helped Gran backstage when she was doing her plays. There were lots of sparkly costumes and actors rushing to and fro. That was great fun. But it's different now – Gran is asking me to perform *on stage*. I want to help her save the theatre but I just don't think I can do it. I have that nervous feeling again, that one like before you have to go to the dentist or take a test.

Pamela is quite good at acting – or, at least, she is very loud and shouty and she waves her arms around a lot. But she is also very excited that she's the star of the show, and she has spent the last ten minutes arguing with Gran about her dressing room.

"Where are the flowers for my dressing room?" Pamela shouts. "My dressing room is so small and dark it looks like a broom cupboard!"

Gran smiles kindly. "Pamela, love," she says, "your dressing room *is* a broom cupboard. We've always shared dressing rooms before.

The only space I could find where you could be on your own was the broom cupboard. I still don't really know what you need it for."

Pamela looks very upset. "I need my own space so that I can prepare," she sniffs. "You know that I need to do my warm-up exercises in private. I have to get my voice ready for the performance."

"Is that what those noises were?" Norman scratches his head. "I thought there was a stray cat stuck in one of the pipes."

"How dare you?" Pamela cries, and flicks the pink feather boa that is wrapped around her neck. "I just don't know how an artist like myself is supposed to perform in these conditions, I really don't." Pamela claps a hand to her head and staggers, then she swoons into a nearby folding chair as if it is all too much for her.

"Hello, all! Sorry I'm late! I – AGH!" someone calls out from the back of the theatre, and suddenly there is a loud thud.

"Not again!" Norman groans.

"I'm all right!" the person shouts, and when I turn round I can see a tall man getting up from the heap he has fallen into.

"Oh dear!" I shout as I jump out of my chair. "Are you OK?"

"Don't worry about him," Denise clucks. "Derek is always falling over, aren't you, Derek?"

The man called Derek gives me a smile. "It's true," he sighs. "I am so terribly clumsy. Always have been. I just tripped over something."

Gran tries to get everyone back to their rehearsal, but Freda and Pamela get into another fight about who can sing the best and the others all have to start taking sides.

I think it's time to have a look around, so I climb the steps up onto the stage. I'd better see what it's like up there – see if it's as scary as I think.

The red curtains are pulled across because so far the rehearsal has been happening on the little bit of stage in front of them. *What's behind those curtains?* I think to myself. It's time to find out.

I tug one curtain back and slip softly through the gap. It's a bit dark back here behind the curtains, and quiet – I can't hear all the actors arguing any more. It gets even more quiet as I step deeper into the gloom.

There are bits of scenery propped up in the dark – trees in a magical forest. Someone has painted little squirrels sitting in the branches and I can see bits of blue sky peeping through at the top. I keep walking and there are more and more painted trees.

Strange, I think. I didn't realise the stage was going to be this big. The scenery is stacked on both sides and I move down the middle like I'm in a tunnel. It's almost as if the trees are getting more and more real. I could have sworn

that squirrel's tail just twitched. And is that ...
a bird singing?

I start to feel scared, so I turn to go back,
but the trees seem to have closed in behind me.
There's a path off to the left and I dash down
it. The gap through the trees twists and turns
and I start to run, my heart thumping. At last,
the trees begin to thin out. I can hear people
talking again.

I trip and reach out with my hand to grab
at the heavy red curtain and pull it aside. I fall
out onto the front of the stage and back into the
light. I'm lying flat out on the floor and panting
hard.

"Ah, Callie," says someone in a squeaky
voice. "*There* you are. It's about time. You're
very, very late." But I can't tell who's talking to
me – it's not anyone I know.

Chapter 3

A Very Smart Mouse

"AGGGGGGGH!" I yell.

"AGGGGGGGH!" yells the little squeaky voice. "Why are you screeching like that? You almost gave me a heart attack."

"Because ... because you're a MOUSE!" I tell him.

The mouse looks at me like I'm an idiot. "Well, of course I am," he says. "I'm Nigel and I'm the stage manager."

He is a very dashing mouse, with white fur and a bright green waistcoat. The waistcoat has teeny tiny gold buttons winking on it. I shake my head, trying to take it in. I close my eyes for a second and then open them.

The mouse is still there. Looking at me with his head tipped to one side.

"Are you OK?" Nigel says, and his whiskers quiver. "Oh, please don't tell me you're ill!

Madame Malone would be so cross. There's no one to be your understudy – no one to step in if you can't perform. If you're ill, we won't be able to put on our play."

"Your … your play?" I say. I don't know what he's talking about. Perhaps I hit my head. Perhaps this is all a strange dream. But it doesn't feel like a dream – it feels very real.

Nigel is still looking worried. He reaches out and puts a paw on my hand. "Do you need a glass of water?" He frowns. "You really don't look very well."

"No, thank you," I murmur, looking around. I'm back in the theatre now, but it looks different. It is clean and bright. The deep red velvet of the seats looks new and plush, the ceiling is painted with a beautiful gold design and an enormous glass chandelier hangs there. The crystals that dangle from it send little rainbows of light twinkling around the room.

"What ... what's happened?" I ask. "Why does the theatre look so good?"

"It does look wonderful, doesn't it?" Nigel says. He sounds very pleased with himself. "I try to take very good care of it. But then, it is a local treasure. An important historical monument."

"That's what Gran says," I say as I get to my feet and dust myself off.

"Well, this *gran* is a very clever animal." Nigel says the word *gran* like he's never heard it before.

"Gran's not an animal!" I cry. "She's a human!"

"A human!" Nigel sounds surprised. "Well, we don't see many of those around here – apart from you of course," he adds politely.

"What do you mean?" I ask. "Where *is* Gran? She was here just a minute ago, right by the stage, over there." I point with a shaky finger.

"Oh dear," Nigel sighs. "You *are* ill. I knew it. This play has just had one disaster after another." He rubs his hands together and looks very upset. "Oh dear, oh dear," he says. "I don't think Madame Malone is going to be very pleased when she hears about this."

"When I hear about what?" someone says from behind us.

I swing around and gasp when I see a fox walking towards me on her two back legs. The fox is wearing a monocle, and I notice that she has very shiny white teeth. She is also wearing a snazzy red jacket and a yellow scarf.

"Well, Nigel." The fox peers at us through her monocle. "What's the latest problem?"

Chapter 4

Meet Madame Malone!

"Ahhh, Madame Malone!" Nigel squeaks. "There's no problem, no problem at all!" he says quickly. "It's just that Callie here was feeling a bit unwell, but she's OK now, aren't you, Callie?" Nigel gives me a worried look.

"Er ... yes," I reply. "I'm fine." I don't want Nigel to get into trouble.

"Excellent," Madame Malone says as she looks hard at me through her monocle. "We wouldn't want anything to happen to our star, would we?"

"Your star?" I say. I frown. What's going on?

"Of course you are our star," Madame Malone says, and she sounds as if she's getting cross. "The play is called *The All-Singing, All-Dancing Tale of Stinky Malone*, and you," Madame Malone points at me, "are playing Stinky Malone. That makes you the star."

"Now, wait just a minute!" I say, and my head starts to spin. "What are you talking about? I'm not in any play! I don't even know where I am! Where is my gran?!" My voice is getting louder and louder.

Madame Malone takes a large white handkerchief from her pocket and then she reaches for her monocle and gives it a good polish. She puts the monocle back in place. "What," she asks finally, "is a *gran*?"

"It seems that a gran is another kind of human," Nigel explains. "Callie seems very upset to have lost the gran."

"She's not *the* gran," I say, and I try not to cry. "She's *my* gran. And I haven't lost her, she was right here in the theatre, or ..." I look round, "maybe not this theatre exactly, but another one that was like it." I stop talking. *Where am I?* I don't understand and I'm starting to worry.

"I see," Madame Malone says at last after a long silence. Her eyes twinkle in a way that makes me think that maybe she really does understand what is going on. "You came through the forest, did you? And you want to go home?"

"Yes, yes!" I nod.

"I can arrange that," Madame Malone says with a friendly smile that shows off her teeth. Her teeth are very white and big but not at all scary. In fact, they remind me of someone, but I can't think who.

"You can?" I say, feeling much better.

"Madame Malone can fix anything," Nigel pipes up. "She *is* our director after all."

"But you will need to do something for me first," the fox says now, and her smile grows even bigger.

"What?" I ask.

"Before I send you home, you need to do an important job for us." Madame Malone is really enjoying herself now.

"What job?" I ask.

"You need to help us save the theatre, of course!" Madame Malone smiles her big smile again. "You need to take on the starring role of Stinky Malone in our play ... Tonight!"

"But – but – I can't!" I stutter. "I can't be in a play in front of people! I just want to go home!"

And then I really do start to cry and I rush off the stage and jump down into the rows of red velvet seats.

"Callie! Stop!" Nigel squeaks.

But I just keep running.

Chapter 5

Save Our Theatre!

I run all the way to the back of the big theatre, past all the rows and rows of seats. I push through the grand swinging gold doors at the back and find myself in the foyer. It's empty. There are stands that sell all sorts of delicious treats, but they are closed at the moment. Beautiful signs hang above them saying:

POPCORN!
CANDYFLOSS!
PEANUTS!
ICE CREAM!

Even the sight of all those delicious words doesn't cheer me up. It's all just too strange and I want to be back with my gran and her friends.

I spy another door and push through it. It opens onto a corridor and I hurry along. The walls are covered with posters of other plays that have been on at the theatre.

WELCOME TO THE WORLD-FAMOUS MADAME MALONE'S MUSIC HALL! the posters say. I stop to look at one of them more closely. It shows a group of actors on stage in their costumes, but the thing that's really strange about it is that all of the actors are animals. Every single one of them. There's Madame Malone the fox in the middle, but next to her is an elephant in a dress! And a hedgehog wearing a feathered hat! And is that ... a giraffe?! I blink and shake my head. This is really strange.

The posters are hung along all the walls, and I keep on walking further and further down the long corridor. I walk for such a long time that I start to worry I'll never reach the end. Finally, I spy a door and I run towards it.

Next to the door is one last picture in a frame, but this one is different from the others. It is some writing from a newspaper.

SAVE OUR THEATRE! the headline says in bold black letters. I read a bit more:

> Madame Malone's Music Hall is
> being torn down! Help us to save
> this historic landmark! Join us
> for a special performance of *The
> All-Singing, All-Dancing Tale of Stinky
> Malone*. All proceeds will go towards
> keeping the theatre open.

I shake my head. This is all getting stranger and stranger. Madame Malone's theatre is going to be closed down, just like Gran's theatre. I feel sad at the thought. The theatre is so very beautiful and all of the pictures on the walls make it look like there have been lots of really good plays here. The theatre must mean a lot to people. I know Gran's theatre means a lot to her, and I have plenty of happy memories of my own from being there. It really would be awful if it was gone for ever.

I push open the door in front of me and then I sigh. How have I ended up here again?

I am at the back of the stage next to the dressing rooms. High over my head hang lights and ropes and scenery waiting to be lowered down.

"There you are, Callie!" Nigel says with a friendly squeak. He's there waiting for me, next to one of the ropes. "I was getting worried about you," he says.

"I can't seem to find my way out of the theatre," I huff. "I am just going in circles."

Nigel pats my leg with his little paw. "Why would you want to leave the theatre?" he asks. "It's the most beautiful, special place in the world."

"It is very beautiful," I agree. "But I think I would still like to go home."

"Well." Nigel tips his head to one side. "Madame Malone says she will help you get home, and Madame Malone always tells the truth."

"So I suppose I have to play Stinky Malone then," I say. "And Madame Malone said the play was tonight!" I've got that horrible nervous feeling in my tummy. "I've never even heard of Stinky Malone!" I yelp as I start to panic. It's bad enough being asked to play Cinderella, but at least I know the story. This is terrible.

"Never heard of Stinky Malone?" Nigel squeaks in shock.

Chapter 6

An Odd Group

"Did she just say she's never heard of Stinky Malone?" a low voice grumbles nearby. It's the hedgehog from the photographs in the corridor! And he looks very grumpy. "This is a disaster!" The hedgehog throws his little arms up in the air. I see that he is wearing a very nice green hat with a long feather in the brim.

"Never heard of Stinky Malone!" a nervous voice says, and a giraffe pops his head around the curtain. He bumps his head on one of the lights. "Ouch!" he cries.

There is a *Thump! Thump! Thump!* noise and then an elephant in a tutu twirls onto the stage. She wears a pink feather boa around her neck. "Do you mean to tell me," she yells dramatically, "that the girl who is playing the part of Stinky Malone doesn't even know the story of Stinky Malone?" The elephant dances on tiptoe to a nearby chair and swoons into it. "Why, oh why aren't I the star?" she sniffs, and her long trunk flicks her feather boa with a swish.

"Now, now, Pansy." Madame Malone arrives and puts a paw on Pansy the elephant's arm. "If you played the part of Stinky Malone, then who would play the part of Princess Sparkles? Who else has the grace? The talent? The style to pull off such a role?"

With each word, Pansy looks happier and happier. "I suppose you are right," she sighs. "I do bring a certain something to my performance."

"And the rest of you," Madame Malone looks at the prickly hedgehog and the nervous giraffe. "Well, you should be helping Callie to prepare, not making her feel bad." The fox flashes her wide toothy smile and everyone looks like they feel a bit better.

"Sorry, Callie," the giraffe says. "I'm Timothy and I'll be happy to help you."

"Me too," grumbles the hedgehog. Madame Malone gives him a little prod. "Oh, yes," the hedgehog mutters, "I'm Gary. Nice to meet you." His voice is still grumpy, but the smile he gives me is quite sweet, even a little bit kind.

"And where are Margo and Doris?" Madame Malone asks.

"Here we are!" call two voices, and a pair of squawking chickens appear. One chicken is wearing a pearl necklace and the other a pair of large red spectacles.

"Margo wouldn't stop going on about her costume," says the chicken with the necklace.

"And Doris just wants to hog all the best bits for herself," clucks the chicken with the glasses, and ruffles her feathers.

"That's quite enough arguing." Madame Malone claps her paws together. "It's time to tell Callie the tale of Stinky Malone."

Everyone sits down in a circle and it's quite nice, like being little at school when the teacher tells you a story.

"Once upon a time, long ago, there lived a clever fox called Stinky Malone," Madame Malone begins.

"Hey!" I cry. "That's your name!" I don't know why I hadn't thought about that before, but then there's been a lot going on.

Madame Malone nods. "Of course," she says. "Stinky was my great-great-great-great-great-grandmother."

"Now stop talking and listen," Pansy says with a cross toot from her trunk.

"Sorry," I reply.

Chapter 7

The Tale of Stinky Malone

"As I was saying," Madame Malone goes on with her story now that everyone is listening. "Once upon a time, long ago, there lived a clever fox called Stinky Malone. Stinky was the sort of fox who liked to help people, but she always seemed to get into trouble herself."

"There was the time she tried to bake a cake for Princess Sparkles' birthday," Pansy the elephant says, "but she mixed up the ingredients."

"Let me guess," I say, "she used salt instead of sugar?"

"Don't be silly!" Pansy laughs. "Salt is delicious. No, by mistake Stinky put in *gunpowder* instead of sugar, and when they lit the candles ... BOOM! Cake everywhere!"

"And gunpowder doesn't even taste nice," grumbles Gary the hedgehog.

"And there was the time she planted those magic beans, hoping they'd grow into treasure for all her friends," puts in Timothy the giraffe. "And a huge beanstalk grew out of the ground."

"Was there an angry giant at the top?" I guess.

"An angry giant?" Margo the chicken looks shocked. "That really would be terrible!"

"No, no," clucks Doris, the other chicken, "the problem was the beans of course. Just think how many beans you get off a giant beanstalk! There were millions. Everyone had to eat beans for every meal. They were drowning in beans!"

"And you know the trouble with beans."
Timothy wrinkles his brow. "Too much wind,"
he whispers.

"Toot! Toot!" Pansy trumpets through her
trunk, and I giggle.

"No wonder she was called Stinky Malone!"
I say, and the others laugh too.

"Yes, Stinky had her fair share of disasters,"
Madame Malone agrees. "She started to feel like
she could never do anything right. But then one
day another fox came to town. His name was
Peppy Twinset and he wasn't like Stinky. He
didn't care a bit about helping others. He only
wanted to help himself."

"Booooooo!" cry the other actors.

"Peppy was always looking for some new
way to make money. He cared about money
more than anything else. More than friends,
or family, or even cake. He didn't care how he

got the money or whom he had to hurt. When Peppy Twinset met Princess Sparkles, he began to plot. He knew that the castle that Princess Sparkles lived in was very valuable. He wanted to buy the castle for himself, but Princess Sparkles wouldn't sell it to him."

"Peppy told her the castle was old and falling down. He said he would be doing her a favour by buying the old wreck off her." Nigel sniffs.

"But Princess Sparkles loved the castle," Madame Malone sighs. "She grew up in it. It was special. She didn't worry about a few bits that didn't look perfect. So Peppy hatched a wicked plan, but he hadn't counted on one person ..."

"STINKY MALONE!" everyone cries.

"That's right." Madame Malone nods. "He hadn't counted on Stinky Malone."

Chapter 8

Stinky Saves the Day

"Stinky Malone had a feeling that Peppy Twinset might be bad news," Madame Malone goes on. "So she decided to keep an eye on him."

"And it was a good job she did!" squeaks Nigel.

"Yes." Madame Malone nods. "Because one day Stinky hid behind a tree and saw Peppy doing something to force Princess Sparkles out of her castle!"

I gasp. "What do you mean? What was Peppy doing?"

"You won't believe it," Pansy says, her trunk twisting in outrage. "But he was trying to knock out some of the stones in the castle so one of the turrets would fall down. Princess Sparkles couldn't pay for repair work, so if the turrets fell down, she'd have to sell the castle to Peppy. The problem was that the stones wouldn't budge. And Stinky overheard him talking to himself. He was trying to work out what evil plan to think up next."

"It's lucky Stinky heard him," I say.

"Oh yes," Nigel nods. "Especially for the people watching our play."

"But what was his evil plan?" I ask.

"Peppy was going to come back that night with some gunpowder and blow the tower up!"

"No!" I cry. "So what did Stinky do?"

"Well, she came up with a very cunning plan." Madame Malone smiles a cunning foxy smile. "Stinky crept away before Peppy saw her, and then she went to tell her friends what she had just seen. They were very angry and they wanted to go and shout at Peppy and tell him to leave the castle alone. But Stinky had a much better idea."

"At first the others weren't sure, because Stinky's ideas always went wrong," says Doris.

"But then, when Stinky explained, everyone agreed it was a very good plan." Margo shakes her feathers.

"Stinky asked everyone to meet back at the tower that night and she told them all to bring their bed sheets with them. When Peppy crept out of the shadows with his torch, Stinky and her friends began to make spooky noises." Madame Malone's voice is very soft now and we all want to hear the story.

"Wooooooooo!" Gary throws his arms up in the air.

"Woooooo!" The others join in.

Madame Malone cuts through their hooting. "'Who is there?!' Peppy cried when he heard all the spooky sounds, but no one answered.

Peppy shook his head and started rolling a small barrel of gunpowder nearer to the castle. 'Wooooooo!' cried the voices again. This time Peppy froze in fright. 'Who is there?!' he asked again. And then Stinky and her friends stepped out from behind the trees where they were hiding. They were all wearing their bed sheets so that they looked like ghosts! Peppy screamed and started to run away, but then one of the ghosts tripped and her sheet slipped off."

"Oh no!" I say.

"That's right," Madame Malone agrees. "It was Stinky. And Peppy started to laugh at her. He said, 'I know all about you, Stinky Malone! All of your plans always go wrong and this one is no different. You've let your friends down again. I bet they wish you'd stop trying to help them!' And with that, he lit the fuse on the gunpowder!"

Everyone who's listening to Madame Malone's story gasps. They all know the story already, but they are leaning forward as if they can't wait to hear the rest.

"The fuse burned as if it was in slow motion," Madame Malone says, "and the animals watched in horror, frozen to the spot. 'Nooooo!' cried Princess Sparkles. 'My lovely castle!' And Peppy only laughed a horrible laugh. 'If I can't have this castle, then no one can!' he said as the last bit of the fuse burned away. The animals all ducked for cover, waiting for the sound of the blast." Madame Malone lifts her paw and the room goes so quiet you could hear a pin drop. "But the sound of the blast never came."

"What happened?" I ask.

"That's just what Peppy said," smirks Madame Malone, "and then everyone looked at Stinky. She smiled. 'Oh dear,' she said. 'It looks as though you've muddled up the gunpowder and the brown sugar. It's an easy mistake to make.' And the animals all cheered for Stinky Malone, who saved the day!"

"Do you mean Stinky swapped the gunpowder with brown sugar?" I ask.

"Yes," Madame Malone says. "Stinky knew that all her mistakes were just lessons that she could learn from. And she knew she was never, ever going to stop trying to help people. Because she'd muddled up gunpowder with brown sugar before, when she had made her cake, she knew what to do to trick Peppy and stop his evil plans."

Madame Malone sits back as the others all cheer. "The end," she says in a very happy voice.

Chapter 9

The Cake Went Boom!

"Now, let's get on with the rehearsal, shall we?" Madame Malone claps her paws together and pats her red coat. "We need to make sure we are all ready for the big performance."

I feel very nervous when Madame Malone says that. "But I don't know what I have to do!" I say. I know the story of Stinky Malone now, but I don't know how to act it out for other people.

"Here's your script," squeaks Nigel, and he holds out a book of white pages all stapled together. "I have marked your lines with a purple pen."

I flick through the pages and see an awful lot of purple pen. "I can't do this!" I cry in panic.

"Oh yes you can," Madame Malone says firmly, "and after you do, then you'll be able to go home."

For a second, Gran's face swims in front of my eyes. I hope she is all right. I hope she isn't worried about me. "OK," I sigh, trying to sound brave. "I will do my best."

"That's all anyone can ask for," Nigel squeaks.

"It's going to be wonderful!" says Pansy as she twirls across the stage.

"Oooof!" says Timothy as he crashes into the scenery.

"Just remember how brave Stinky was," Madame Malone says, looking right at me. "If she can do it, so can you."

"You're right," I say, and I stand up tall. "I just need to be more like Stinky!"

"That's the spirit!" Margo clucks.

I take a deep breath. "Let's get started."

*

"And the cake went BOOM! The cake went BOOM! Oh, that is when the cake went BOOOOOOOOM!" we all sing in our best voices as Nigel hammers away at a very small piano. I must admit that the songs are very catchy, and I wiggle from side to side, trying to copy some of the dance moves I've been taught.

Pansy tap-dances across the stage, her feather boa flapping behind her.

A pink feather floats off the boa and flies gently through the air towards Timothy's nose. Oh no! I have a feeling I know what's going to happen next.

"AH-AH-AH-CHOOO!" Timothy sneezes an enormous sneeze, and his long knobbly legs tremble. He falls forward and bangs into Gary's hedgehog spikes.

"AGH!" Timothy screeches, and trips over. He grabs at the red velvet curtain with his teeth to pull himself up, but instead there's a ripping sound and the curtain and Timothy both come crashing down to the ground. Timothy sprawls on the floor, his four legs going out in all directions, and he skids across the stage, dragging the ripped curtain with him.

"THE SHOW MUST GO ON!" Pansy yells loudly, with a huge smile stuck across her face and still tap-dancing so fast her feet are a blur. "DON'T LOSE FOCUS!" Pansy starts to twirl

around and around, and then she knocks into a small black box that sits at the side of the stage.

Almost at once a small cloud of smoke comes out of it.

"Is something on fire?" I hiss, and I look at Gary, who is frozen in panic. He can't remember his next line.

The smoke gets thicker and thicker so that it's curling all around us.

"IS SOMETHING ON FIRE?" I ask more loudly.

"It's just the smoke machine," Pansy whispers. "Keep going."

But the smoke is now filling the stage. No one can see where they're going.

"OOF!" comes a voice. Then there's a crash and a lot of bangs that get louder and louder.

"THAT'S MY WING YOU'RE PINCHING!" I hear Doris squawk.

"Terribly sorry," comes Timothy's voice.

"Oh, the cake went boom!" I sing, still trying to do my dance moves as the cloud of smoke gets even thicker so that I can't see anything at all.

The hacking, honking sound of animals coughing fills the air.

"CUT!" Madame Malone's voice cries from somewhere in the darkness. "I think we'd better stop there."

Chapter 10

Madame Malone Needs Help

When at last the smoke clears, no one can see Madame Malone.

While all the animals are arguing about who made the biggest mess of the rehearsal, I sneak off to try to find her.

When I do spy her, she is sitting in one of the dressing rooms. She is holding her monocle in her paws and her claws make a sharp tap-tap-tap sound on the glass. She is thinking hard, and for once no one can see her big shiny teeth, because she is definitely not smiling. In fact, I think she looks a little bit sad.

She looks up and sees me.

"Ah, Callie," she says. She tries to sound cheerful.

"Can I come in?" I ask.

"Of course." Madame Malone points to a chair across from her. "Please, have a seat."

I curl up in the comfy pink chair. "I think this must be Pansy's dressing room."

"You're right there." She chuckles softly. "How did you know?"

I look around at the pink furniture, the pink twinkly lights hanging from the ceiling and the wall of pink feather boas all hanging neatly from their hooks. "Just a guess," I smile.

We both sit there without saying anything. Madame Malone begins to play with her monocle again. She seems worried.

"Is everything all right?" I ask.

Madame Malone sighs.

"Is it about the rehearsal?" I ask. "I know it was a bit of a disaster, but I'm sure we can get better." I'm actually *not* that sure, but I want to try to sound positive.

"In a way," she says. She turns to look at me. "What do you know about this theatre?" she asks as she looks all round her.

"I saw the newspaper article," I say. "I know they're going to close it down."

Madame Malone sighs again. "It's been in my family for many, many years, you know."

"It's a beautiful theatre," I murmur.

"It is." She dips her head. "But it's not about how beautiful it is, not really. It's about how much people love it, how they depend on it.

People come here to escape, they come here to laugh and be happy. The actors as well as the audience. It means a lot to them. It means a lot to all of us."

"Like the castle in the play we're doing?" I say, starting to understand.

"Exactly." Madame Malone nods and smiles. "Just like that. How Princess Sparkles feels about her castle is how I feel about this place. I grew up here."

"That's the same as my gran." I lean forward and rest my elbows on my knees. "She loves her old theatre like that. She's trying to save it too."

"Well," Madame Malone says. "I hope she has better luck than us." She shakes her head. "I thought telling the story of Stinky Malone would be a great way to raise the money we need to save the theatre, but so far there's been one disaster after another."

She looks so sad that it makes something inside me hurt too. I don't like seeing her like this. Madame Malone has always seemed so tough and in charge.

I sit up straight. "Well, Stinky Malone had one disaster after another," I say, "but she saved the day in the end."

Madame Malone gives a tiny smile. "You're right," she says slowly. "We shouldn't give up."

"Definitely not!" I cry as I jump to my feet. "Because if there's anything I've learned from Stinky it's that if your friends need your help, then you have to be right there to help them!"

Chapter 11

Callie to the Rescue

When I leave the dressing room where I've been chatting with Madame Malone, I feel strong and brave again. I may not have known these animals for long, but I like them. They're funny and friendly, and they are trying to save the theatre that means so much to them.

I feel a bit sorry too. It took the story of Stinky Malone for me to see how much Gran's theatre means to her and her friends. I should have been more helpful. I make myself a promise that if ... no, WHEN I get home, I will help Gran to save her favourite place.

"One theatre at a time, Callie," I murmur to myself. "Let's get this sorted first."

*

The animals are still arguing.

"But I don't see why you get to be the one to wear the orange feathers," Margo is screeching at Doris.

"And I don't see why Gary can't remember any of his lines," Pansy huffs, and looks down her trunk at the hedgehog.

"I *can* remember my lines!" Gary tells her crossly.

"He just gets a bit of stage fright," Timothy says kindly.

"No, I do not!" Gary blusters. "It's just that you're always falling over and I forget what

I'm meant to say. We never know what awful accident you're going to cause next!"

"Don't take it out on Timothy, just because *you're* nervous!" Doris clucks.

"I think we are *all* nervous," I say. I step forward and everyone stops talking.

The animals all look at me as if they are waiting for something. I take a deep breath. "You all love this theatre, don't you?" I ask.

They nod. Pansy sniffs a little bit.

"And you all want to save it. So of course you are all feeling nervous, of course things keep going wrong. It's an awful lot of pressure." I keep my voice soft.

"It *is* a lot of pressure!" Pansy says, and her lips wobble. "Madame Malone's Music Hall has been like our home for years now. We all love it so much, and if we can't pull off this performance, then they're going to sell it and tear it downnnnnn!"

The last word is a wail as Pansy starts to cry. Nigel hurries over and pulls a clean white handkerchief out of his waistcoat and hands it to her. Pansy blows her trunk with a squeaky *toot, toot*!

"Well, we're not going to let that happen," I say firmly. "Think about the story of Stinky Malone. That's all about how Stinky helps to save the castle from being destroyed."

"You're right!" Timothy cries. "I hadn't thought about that, but the way Princess Sparkles feels about the castle is how we all feel about the theatre."

I nod. "But the most important thing in the story isn't the castle at all," I say, and the animals all lean forward to listen. "The important thing is that Princess Sparkles has good friends who want to help her."

"Good friends like Stinky!" Doris puts in.

"That's right," I agree. "And I know someone who needs you all to start behaving more like friends."

"Madame Malone!" Nigel squeaks. "She needs us!" He says the words as if he can hardly believe them.

"If Madame Malone needs us, then we must help her!" Gary stands up as tall as he can. "We have to save this play, and we have to save the theatre. For Madame Malone, and for the theatre, and for all of us!"

The animals all cheer.

"Well, thank you, everyone." A voice comes from nearby and Madame Malone steps out from behind the curtain. "I'm very happy to hear you say that." She smiles her big toothy smile. "So, let's get back to rehearsals, shall we?"

Chapter 12

The Big Performance

"I think I'm going to be sick," I say a few hours later. I'm wearing my costume – dungarees and a green and red striped shirt, with a pair of beautiful red fox ears made out of soft velvet. Nigel has carefully painted whiskers on my cheeks.

"It's perfectly normal to get nervous," Pansy says.

"Y-y-yes," Gary says, but his teeth are chattering. "P-p-perfectly normal."

When I see how nervous Gary is too, I feel a bit better. "Oh, please don't worry, Gary," I say as I pat him very gently so that I don't get hurt on his spikes. "You did so well in rehearsal; you remembered all of your lines! You can do this!"

"Callie is right," Timothy puts in. "You were wonderful. There's no need to be afraid."

"They're starting to come in!" Doris clucks loudly. "It's sold out! There's hundreds of them!"

"Ohhhhh!" moans Gary, going a bit green.

I feel my own tummy swoop and spin around inside me. I go and have a peek through the curtains and then I wish I hadn't. There really are hundreds of animals out there, all filling up the seats and chatting noisily.

"Ohhhhh!" I moan softly, sounding just like Gary. Then someone puts an arm around me.

"Don't worry, Callie," Madame Malone says gently. "You just do your best and they'll all love you."

"But I don't want to let you down!" I whisper.

Madame Malone looks surprised. "Let me down!" she says, "Why, Callie, you could never do that! You've already made such a difference. You've helped all of us to believe in ourselves. We wouldn't be able to do any of this without you." She smiles at me and I feel better.

"Places, everyone!" Nigel's voice squeaks from behind me.

"Break a leg!" Madame Malone says, and then she looks over at Timothy. "That means good luck," she explains. "Don't really break anything, please!" She chuckles and I laugh too, but my laugh comes out a bit wheezy and nervous.

I move to the side of the stage as if I'm in a dream. "You can do it, Callie!" Nigel whispers in the darkness beside me. I look down and see him giving me a tiny thumbs up. I take a deep breath. He's right. I can do this. I will do it. And then, with a slight creaking noise, the curtains start to part and the lights go up on the stage, and I have no more time to worry because the play is starting!

And as soon as it does start, my nerves seem to melt away. It's as if the world shrinks away and all I can think about is what I'm doing right now.

I can hear the audience – they cheer and laugh as we perform, but thanks to the bright stage lights I can't see them. I say the words that we've been practising all day, and I begin to feel almost like I actually *am* Stinky Malone.

I look around at my new friends and I feel my heart glow in my chest. Gary remembers all of his lines, Doris and Margo make everyone laugh, Timothy doesn't have a single accident, and Pansy is perfect as Princess Sparkles, dancing across the stage, her lovely tiara shining and sparkling on top of her head.

We sing and dance, and I suddenly realise that this is the most fun I've had in ages. I understand now why all the animals want to fight to keep the theatre alive – it's because it makes everyone so happy. Not just us but the audience too. When we sing the final line of the final song, we stand in a row ready to take our bows and the clapping and the cheers go on and on and on. The lights in the audience come up so we can finally see them and there's Madame Malone in the front row, clapping and cheering as loudly as anyone, with an enormous grin on her face.

I see her mouth move and I can read the words there: "Thank you."

Chapter 13

There's No Place Like Home

The hooting and hollering from the audience goes on and on and we take our bows.

"Stinky! Stinky!" the crowd chant, and they are all on their feet. Gary pushes me forward to the front of the stage as the cheering gets louder and louder – a roar that fills my ears. I am smiling so hard that my face hurts. I bow again and when I stand up the light that shines in my face is so bright that I have to lift my hand to cover my eyes.

The sound from the crowd has turned into a sort of whooshing noise, and the lights just keep on getting brighter and brighter. I squeeze my eyes shut.

Then, just like that, the noise stops. Everything is silent. I open one eye slowly, and then the other.

"Oh!" I say, because now there's no audience at all. No sparkling chandelier, no animals. Instead I'm back at the old theatre, and I'm so happy to see it.

"There you are, Callie!" someone says. "We've been looking all over for you!"

"Gran!" I screech, running to her and throwing myself into her arms. Gran's hug wraps around me like a snuggly jumper.

"What's this for?" Gran asks.

"I'm just happy to see you," I say.

"Well, that's nice." Gran pats me on my arm and gives me a big smile, one that shows off all her big white teeth, and for a second I almost think I'm looking at Madame Malone.

"How's the rehearsal going?" I ask.

Gran sighs. "Between you and me, dear, it's hard work being a director. This lot need a good talking-to."

"Maybe I can help," I grin.

"You?" Gran is surprised. "I didn't really think this was your cup of tea, love. I know you don't want to be on stage; I'm sorry that I asked you to do it. You don't need to do anything you don't feel happy about."

"Oh, but I *do* want to do it," I say as I look around at the theatre. "I didn't understand before, but I do now. This place is special. We have to do everything we can to save it." I think about Nigel the mouse and his proud, whiskery face. "We have to make it look beautiful!" I add.

"That's the spirit!" Gran cheers. "So, do you have any ideas?"

"Well, I do have one," I say with a smile. "Let me ask you, have you ever heard of *The All-Singing, All-Dancing Tale of Stinky Malone*?"

Gran shakes her head. "No, dear, I can't say that I have."

"Well, gather the troops!" I cry, rubbing my hands together. "Because I have a story to tell you all, and you're going to love it ..."

Our books are tested
for children and young people by
children and young people.

Thanks to everyone who consulted on
a manuscript for their time and effort in
helping us to make our books better
for our readers.